For Mum and Dad
Many thanks for all your support
and in happy memory of Judy
C.F.

To Mummy and Daddy
for all those bits of
cotton on the floor
M.B-H.

First published in the USA in paperback in 2001
by Zero to Ten Ltd.
814 North Franklin Street, Chicago, Illinois 60610

Copyright © Zero to Ten Ltd 1998
Text copyright © Margaret Bateson-Hill 1998
Illustrations copyright © Christine Fowler 1998
Lakota translation copyright © Philomine Lakota 1998

Publisher: Anna McQuinn
Art Director: Tim Foster
Senior Art Editor: Sarah Godwin
Designer: Tiffany Leeson

Library of Congress CIP data applied for.

ISBN 1-84089-023-1

Printed in Hong Kong

The publishers would like to acknowledge the help
of the following people, without whom this project could
never have been developed let alone completed: to Erica
Marcus for her invaluable help and optimism at the outset;
to Kay Karol Horse Capture for recommending *Robes of
Splendour* (especially the chapter by George Horse Capture,
whose insights on the buffalo hide collection in the Musee de
l'Homme inspired both the designer and the artist); to Gloria
for her care and carefulness, her wisdom, her openness and
willingness to share and guide us; to Philomine for her
patience and skill. To the Red Cloud School whose calendar
of star quilts was given to us by Gloria and became the
inspiration behind the quilts in the book; to Shota Olowan,
Gloria's granddaughter, whose beautiful name Margaret
borrowed for the story's heroine; and to Christ Church
School where Margaret tested the collage project and who
have now completed their own quilt with the help
of their teacher, Colette Morris.

Finally, thanks to Margaret and Christine especially for being
patient with us during the project's long evolution.
We think it has been WELL worth the wait.

A small royalty from this book will be paid to the
Freemont County School, District #14, Ethete, Wyoming.

SHOTA

AND THE STAR QUILT

Written by

MARGARET BATESON-HILL

Illustrated by

CHRISTINE FOWLER

Consultant

GLORIA RUNS CLOSE TO LODGE

Lakota text by

PHILOMINE LAKOTA

The hearts of
little children are pure
and therefore the Great Spirit
may show them many things
which older people miss.

Black Elk, 1949

There was once a man who lived at the top of a tower in the middle of a big city. He claimed he had fallen to earth as a shooting star, eager to win the riches and power he had seen in his wanderings of the night sky.

Riches had bought him half of the city, but he had found neither love nor happiness. Every lonely night he would climb to the top of his tower and gaze up at the night sky, remembering the song his mother had sung to him,

Find the star that's a gift from the skies.
In its patchwork of light true happiness lies.

But the star was not to be found and, dropping his gaze earthwards to the happy homes that surrounded his tower, a bitterness filled his heart. The following morning he would send out the order to buy these homes for "development."

Watohan wicasa wan otunwahe cokata tipi wankatiya tiwankata hci ti. Oglakin na wicahpi hinhpaya heca ca maka ta hi keye. Mahpiya tanhan kutakiya wanyanke ki makoce el lila wowajica na wowasake ota hena iyutan na ohiiciya cin un maka ta hi keye.

Wowajica un otunwahe iyokise opeicitun eyas hecina iyokipi sni.

Hanhepi iyohila wicahpi ecetkia etunwe na hunku olowan wan kahiyaye sa kaki kiksuye,

Wicahpi wan nicupi ki he ole ye.
Iyoyamya he ki ohan wowicake na wowiyuskin ki he ye.

Eyas wicahpi he iyeya okihisni. Hokuta kiya etunwe na tiwahe oiyokipiya oksan he ki hena wan wicayanke na lila icanl sice. Tiwahe eya tipi ogna yankapi ki hena iyuha tipi ki opetun kta ca hinhanni ki wonahun wowapi wicaku kte.

In the same city, not far from the Starman's tower, lived two girls called Shota and Esther. They were best friends and had lived next door to one another in an apartment building since Shota's family had moved to the city from the reservation at Pine Ridge, to find work.

Esther had lived in the same apartment all her life with her mother, father, brothers and grandmother. Every day, the girls would meet to play and sometimes they would sit on the stairs and talk. Most of all, the girls liked to sit with Esther's Grandma Elsa and listen to her stories of faraway times and faraway places.

But now the girls were preparing to visit Shota's grandmother, Rose Flying Eagle, for the annual pow-wow. They were very excited; this would be Esther's first visit to Pine Ridge.

Otunwahe ki hel ohan insinyan wicincala num tipi. Wanji Shota eciyapi na unma Esther eciyapi.

Shota ta tiwahe ki Pine Ridge etan otunwahe ta ahitipi. Esther iye tohunya ki otunwahe el hunku na atkuku na tibloku na kunsitku ob ti. Hehantan ti unma el kici kiyela ti pi na lila tanyan maske kiciyapi. Anpetu iyohila wicincala ki skatapi na watohan sna ecela tiopa oiyahe el yankapi na woglakapi. Watohan sna Esther kunsitku Elsa kici yankapi na Unci Elsa ehanni Lakota oyate ki tokel ounyapi oyaka can lila iyokipi pi.

Eyas le anpetu ki Shota kunsitku, Rose Flying Eagle, wanyang yapi na ko wacipi kta ca un igluwinyeyapi. Le otokaheya Esther Pine Ridge ta yin kta ca lila inihan pi na wiyuskin pi.

The day before their journey a letter arrived – the envelope was stamped with a strange picture of a man's face shaped like a star. Shota's father read the letter aloud:

> *Starman Property Development Company has acquired*
> *this apartment building for development. You are hereby given*
> *notice (three months) to vacate these premises.*

He threw the letter onto the table. He was angry and upset. "Yet again we are told to give up our homes – some things never change."

Shota turned to her mother, "Can Mr. Starman take away our homes?"

"Well, he is a rich and powerful man," she replied, "so he probably can." Shota felt her insides go numb. "Can't we do something?" she asked.

"We can organize a petition," said her mother.

"But don't worry and don't let it spoil your vacation."

Pine Ridge ta iyayapi sni hanni anpetu itokab hehan wowapi wan icupi. Wowapi ognake ki el wicasa wan wicahpi owanke ca itowapi. Shota atkuku ki wowapi ki yugan na yawa:

> *Wicahpi Wicasa Tawowasi ki makoce na tipi nakan pi ki*
> *opetun ca letan wi yawapi yamni ki yatipi etan heyap ilala pi kte.*

Shota atkuku ki le yawa na lila canzeke na iyokipi sni. Wowapi ki waglutapi akan ihpeye na heye, "Wasicu ki tohanni tohan glutokcab sni. Ake wasicu ki tiwahe etan hap unyan pelo," eye. Shota hunku ki ayutan na heye, "Wicahpi Wicasa tipi unkib okihihe?" hunku ki ayuptin na heye, "Icin Wicahpi Wicasa ki wijica na wowasake yuha ca hecun okihi ye," eye.

Shota nihinciye un tamahel tata ahi eyas hecina heye, "Takun ecun kum unkokihib he?" hunku ki ayupte na heye, "Tiwahe ki lena wica unyuwita pi kte na wowapi wanji wicaunlapi sni ki un unkoigwa pi kte. Ca le un nagi yeiciye sni ye, na anpetu waste wanji yuha ye!" eye.

Early the next morning the girls were waiting excitedly for Shota's Uncle Joe. He was going home to Pine Ridge for the pow-wow and would take them with him.

There were hugs and kisses and goodbyes, and the girls climbed into the back of his car, ready for the long journey. It was evening when they finally reached the welcoming arms of Rose Flying Eagle.

Shota's grandmother was delighted to have the girls to stay and told Esther to call her "Unci" like Shota did. But her happiness soon turned to anger when they told her the terrible news.

"When will these powerful men come to recognize the suffering they inflict? I wonder if they'll ever learn?"

Then she smiled. "But we can talk about this in the morning. Now it's time for bed."

Ihinhanni el wicincala ki lila wiyuskin pi na Shota leksitku Joe apepi. Joe Pine Ridge ta waci yin kta ca kici yapi kte. Wanna iyehantu ca poskaska okiciyuspa pi na Joe ta iyecinkainyanka lazatan han iyotakapi. Pine Ridge lila otehan ca tehan yapi kte.

Htayetu el Pine Ridge ta ihunnipi na Shota kunsitku Rose Flying Eagle kici iyokipiya wankici yankapi. Esther insinyan Unci Rose ekiye si na lila Unci Rose iyokipi. Eyas hap wicayapi wonahun ki nahun na insinya lila canzeke.

"Wicasa wowasaka yuhapi lena oyate ki tehiya wica kuwapi ki tohan ablezapi kta he?" eye. "Toksa le hinhanni ki iwounglakapi kte. Toeyas wanna iyunkapi kta iyehantu ye," eye Unci Rose.

In the middle of the night Shota was still wide awake. Looking out of the window, she thought, "I must go out and look at the stars!"

Outside, the dark trees held the land in shadow, but as she gazed upwards, the sky became alive with stars, swirling and moving in the intricate patterns of a long-known dance. It was the most beautiful sight she had ever seen. Time stood still as the young girl watched.

Finally she felt cold and she turned to go in. There, laying at her feet, was a flat, white stone. She bent down to pick it up. It was the perfect shape of a diamond and seemed to twinkle and sparkle – like a small fragment from one of the faraway stars dancing high above her.

"Thank you," she whispered up to the night sky. "Oh, thank you."

Hancoka eyas hecina Shota istima okihi sni ca hankeya tankal inape na wicahpi ecetkiya watunwan najin.

Tankal wazi ahanheya he ki un makoce ki oiyokpas ya he. Wankal etunwan najin na wicahpi wanwica yanke. Wicahpi ki iyuha iyoyamya kahomnimniya wacipi selececa. Lila owang waste na owatohan owape ki owanjila he selececa.

Hankeya Shota cuwita ca tima kigni kta yunkan, hokuta kiya wanyan ke ki si ki el inyan wan ska na blaska ca hel yanke. Wicahpi pinkpa ca lila waste na wiyakpakpa yanke.

Shota inyan blaska ki pahi na icu na lila iyokipi. Wankatakiya etunwin na "Lila pilamayape!" eye.

When Shota awoke late the next morning, her night adventure seemed like a dream – but there in her hand was the diamond-shaped stone.

Still holding the stone, she went to find her grandmother and Esther. They were looking at the quilt on Unci's bed.

"Shota has one, just like this, on her bed," she heard Esther saying. "Yes," replied Unci. "It's a star quilt, I gave it to her when she moved because the bright city lights make it so difficult to see the stars..." Suddenly she broke off, "Why Shota, what's the matter?" Shota was staring at the quilt.

"My stone, it's the same as the diamonds – look!" she cried.

She placed the stone on one of the diamonds. It was a perfect fit. Then she told her grandmother about the wonder of the night sky and how she had found the stone lying at her feet. Unci was very quiet and said softly,

"Often in times of great need a member of our family has been given a very special gift. Look after it carefully, Tacoja."

Ihinhanni el Shota kikta na tokins ihambla kecin, yunka inyan blaska ki hecina nape ogna yuha. Hecina inyan ki nape ogna yuha na ta maskeku Esther na kunsitku Rose ekta wicai.

Esther ena kunsitku Rose kici wicahpi owinja wan oyunke el akahpa han ca wanyanka hanpi. Esther heye, "Wicahpi owinja lececa wan Shota ta oyunke el insinyan akahpa kigle," eye. Unci Rose heye, "Han, he wicahpi owinja ki Shota otunwahe ta yin kta ca he waku we. Otunwahe ki iyoyamya he ki un wicahpi wanyanka okihi kte sni ca he un wicahpi owinja he wecicage," eye. Unci Rose ungnahelaka Shota ayuta na tokaki iyunge.

Shota heye, "Inyan ki le wicahpi pinkpa ospula ki iyececa!" eye. Hecun nahan inyan ki wicahpi pinkpa ospula aiyopteya egnake yunka lila yupiya kipi. Toske inyan blaska le iye ki kunsitku Rose okiyake. Unci Rose tagni eye sni inila yanke na heye, "Tohan tehi can tiwahe etan wanji takun waste iye ca tanyan awanyanka ye, Takoja." eye.

"*Now I know* what we must do," said Shota. "We must make a star quilt to celebrate our homes!"

"Oh, yes, Shota!" said Esther, "in the middle we could put the apartment building with us standing outside. It will be perfect."

Unci taught the girls how to cut and sew the diamond pieces. They worked slowly, so Unci asked some friends who were experienced quilt-makers to help. As they worked, the women talked and traded stories. Mary, one of Unci's oldest friends, explained to the girls that star quilts are very special to Lakota families.

"We usually give them on special occasions," she said. "The image of the star goes way back in our people's history."

"Yes," added another woman, "you can even see them on the buffalo hides worn hundreds of years ago."

Unci made the central panel herself and the girls squealed with delight to see themselves sewn in tiny stitches standing outside their apartment building.

"*Wanna* taku tokun kun kte ki slolwaye," eye Shota. "Wicahpi owinja wanji unkaga pi kte heca. Tipi ungluonihanpi un unkagapi kte." Esther heye, "Cokan tipi itankal naunjin unkagapi kte. Hecel waste kte!"

Unci Rose wicahpi owinja yuksaksa na kagege unspe wicakiye. Ehanta wicahpi owinja kaga wopika pi eya wicakico na wicincala ki owicakiye wicakiye. Wanji Mary eciyapi ca he oyakin na wicahpi owinja ki lila Lakota ki tekihila pi keye. Tohunyan ki wicahpi ki Lakota wicoicage hehantan kiksuyapi. Nakun winyan ki wanji oyakin na ehanni tatanka ha ki el sna wicahpi owicawapi keye.

Unci Rose iye iyatayela ocokan he kage. Shota na Esther wan iciglakapi na lila iyokipi pi.

It was soon time to go back to the city and all that was left to do was a border to edge the quilt. When the girls took it out of their bag, everyone loved it – not just Shota and Esther's families. All the neighbors asked to see it! Somebody gave the girls a small piece of cloth for the border, and soon everyone was offering scraps of material.

They decided to make the border out of these small pieces, so everyone would be part of the quilt. So, while the parents arranged a meeting with the Starman Company, the girls organized the sewing.

Neighbors came to help, until the quilt was finished. Everyone stood silently marvelling at it, until Shota's mother spoke.

"Shota and Esther, you have made something very special – this quilt is a mirror of the love shared in our homes. We are very proud of you!" Everybody started cheering and clapping.

"Please Mr. Starman," thought Shota, "don't take this away from us."

Wanna ecanni otunwahe ta gla pi kta iyehantu. Owinja ki ehake ohomni apata pi. Tuwe keyas lila owinja ki yawaste pi na waste lakapi. Oyate ohomni ounyanpi ki iyuha mnihuha ospula kicunpi ca hena un owinja ki ohomni apatapi na yustanpi. Hecel oyate ki iyohila owinja ki kaga pi hel ohan opapi kte.

Wicincala ki hunku pi na atkuku pi ki wowapi yuha skan pi ecunhan insinyan owinja yuha yanka pi na yustan pi. Tuwe keyas itunpa wanyang najin pi nahan Shota hunku ki heye, "Shota na Esther, owinja wan lila waste yakagapi. Wowaste luhapi ki un etanhan tiwahe el owasin wowaste yuhapi." Lila uniyuonihanpi. Tuwe keyas iyokipi pi na awicasa pi na nape glaskapapi. Ecunhan Shota hecin najiin, "Wicahpi Wicasa le ko unki pi sni ye!" ecin.

It was time to present the petition – everyone was anxious. Shota and Esther had decided to bring the quilt. They had carefully folded it, so it would be ready for them to show when the right moment came.

The Starman's tower was very tall and had mirror windows that stopped you looking in. Everyone went inside and Shota's father and the other representatives were shown into a room. But Shota and Esther were firmly told to stay outside. The girls were shocked. How would they be able to show the quilt?

Shota nudged Esther. "We must look for Mr. Starman himself. I bet we'll find his office at the very top of the tower."

Everybody was much too busy to notice two little girls getting into the elevator. They pressed the button for the top floor.

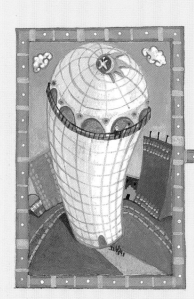

Wanna wowapi he gloapi kta iyehantu. Tuwe keyas nihinciyapi. Shota na Esther okunjila owinja ki wanyankapi. Tanyan pehan yanke. Tohan iyehantu ki owinja ki pazo pi kte.

Wicahpi Wicasa ti ki ta ojanjan glepi ki kakpa wanyanka okihipi sni. Shota atkuku hunh op hena ecela tima ye wicakiyapi. Shota na Esther tankal najin wicasi pi. Wincincala ki tansagtapi. Toske owinja ki he pazo pi kta he, tima ye wicakiya pi sni ca.

Shota Esther panini na heye, "Wicahpi Wicasa ki unkiyecinkala unkole na ekta unyin kte heca. Ti wankatiya heci iyeunyan unkokihi." Tuweni wicincala ki el ewicatunwe sni ca ti wankatakiya iyayapi.

Shota and Esther stepped out into a large room. A man was sitting by the window looking out at the sky. His face was sad and tired, but they noticed how his skin shimmered in the light. Unaware of the two girls, he started to sing,

Find the star that's a gift from the skies.
In its patchwork of light true happiness lies.

They listened in amazement. This song was about their quilt. "Excuse me, Sir," said Esther in her loudest voice. "We've brought you the star – it's here on the quilt!" Together, the two girls held up the quilt. Startled, the Starman leapt from his chair.

When he saw the quilt he stared in wonder – the morning sun streamed in through the window, catching the diamonds of color.

"We made the quilt," said Shota, "to show you how much we love our homes. Please Mr. Starman, don't make us move away."

The Starman stared at the quilt with tear-filled eyes. Finally he spoke.

"So here it is at last – the star where true happiness lies. What great happiness! A home! Family! Friends... I could be happy, if I was surrounded by so much love."

For the first time in his life the Starman understood what he had done. Looking out of the window he saw the endless rows of office buildings that had replaced so many happy homes, and he felt ashamed. Looking at the girls he declared, "I promise not to take away your homes. Now please go away and leave me alone."

Ti wankatiya ihuni pi na Wicahpi Wicasa ki iyeyapi. Ojanjan glepi wan ecetkiya etunwan yankin na lila iyoksice na yugo owanke. Eyas ha ki wiyakpakpa hingle na iyoyamya yanke. Wincincala ki wanwica yanke sni icilowan,

Wicahpi wan nicupi ki he ole ye.

Iyoyamya he ki ohan wowicake na wowiyuskin ki he ye.

Wicincala ki lila inihan anagoptan pi. Wicahpi Wicasa lowan ki le owinja ki le eca ilowanhe. Esther hotanka kicun na wicasa ki okiyake na heye, "Wicahpi wan iyalowanhe ki he le e ye!" eye. Wicahpi Wicasa ki skan hingle na napsilye iciye na lila owinja ki tanyan ablesya wanyanke. Ojanjan glepi etan iyoyamya wicahpi owinja ki owang waste ya he.

Shota heye, "Le owinja ki unkiye unkagapi. Tohan tiwahe teunkihila pi ki un nicipazo pi kta un le unkagapi. Tipi el unyanka pi etan hab unyapi sni ye," eye. Wichapi Wicasa ki lila owinja ki ayutan najin na istamniyam hiyu na heye, "Wicahpi wan el oiyokipiya he ki he le e yelo! Tipi na tiwahe na otakuya na okolaku lena eyelo! Lena mita oksan ounyapi hanta lel iyomakipi owakihi yelo!"

Otokaheya Wicahpi Wicasa ki wan iciglake na aicibleze. Tankal etunwa najin na wanyanke. Oyate tipi na tiwahe yankapi hena lila ota opetun na hab wicaye. Lena wanyanke na lila ikistece. Wicincala ki awicayutan na heye, "Tipi na tiwahe nitawa pi ki etan hab ciya pi kte sni yelo! Wanna gla po na amayustan po!" eye.

But the girls could not
leave this man locked in such
loneliness. Suddenly they knew
what they must do. Carefully
they wrapped the quilt
around the Starman.

"It's for you to keep,"
whispered Esther.

"Maybe it will help you
remember your home," said
Shota. The two girls slipped
silently from the room.

Eyas wincincala ki kigalapi
sni. Wicahpi Wicasa ki lila
iyoksice ki un isnala ayustanpi
okihipi sni. Ungnahelaka
iyukcan pi na wicahpi owinja ki
un Wicahpi Wicasa ki in kiyapi
na aopemni pi na kupi.

"Niye le wicahpi owinja ki
yuha ye," eya okiyakapi. Ungna
un nititakuye wicaye ksuyin kte
sece eyapi. Hecun na inila naslal
kinapapi.

Shota and Esther knew Mr. Starman would keep his promise to them, but it wasn't until the evening that the message came. Their homes were safe. Shota's mother found the girls sitting happily on the stairs.

"You two knew about this, didn't you?" she said. Then she added quietly, "It was Mr. Starman's final order... He's gone."

Shota and Esther looked at each other. What did she mean? Then Shota remembered her stone from the stars and understood – the Starman had gone home. She gazed up at the night sky and there, low on the horizon, was a single, pale star. Softly, Shota began to sing,

> *Find the star that's a gift from the skies,*
> *In its patchwork of light true happiness lies.*

"I hope you find your happiness," whispered Shota.
"I've found mine!"

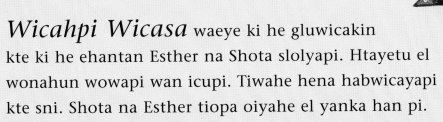

Wicahpi Wicasa waeye ki he gluwicakin kte ki he ehantan Esther na Shota slolyapi. Htayetu el wonahun wowapi wan icupi. Tiwahe hena habwicayapi kte sni. Shota na Esther tiopa oiyahe el yanka han pi.
Shota hunku ki el wicahi na awicayutan. Wicincala ki lila iyokipi pi ca wanyanke.

Shota hunku ki iwicayunge na heye, "Le ehantan slolyapi ce?" eye.
"Le ehake wonahun wowapi ki Wicahpi Wicasa ki kage na tokiya iyaye," eye.

Shota na Esther akiciyutanpi na le taku ke ki lila iyukcanpi. Ungnahelaka Shota kiksuye. Inyan wan wicahpi etan hi ki he eca ke ki ableze. Wicasa Wicahpi ki mahpiya ta kigle. Wankatakiya etunwan yunkan wicahpi wan tokecela iyoyamya yanke. Shota iwastegla inila olowan kicahiyaye,

> *Wicahpi wan nicupi ki he ole ye.*
> *Iyoyamya he ki ohan wowicake na wowiyuskin ki he ye.*

"Esa wowiyuskin eye yakin na iyuskinya yaun ni! Miye wann wowiyuskin eyewaki ye!" Shota heye.

TO MAKE A STAR COLLAGE

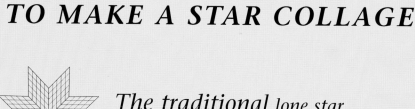

The traditional lone star pattern is an eight-pointed star, made up of 8 large diamonds. Each large diamond is in turn made up of 25 small diamonds. Altogether the star collage has 200 small diamonds.

Each small diamond should be the size of template (a), 4 in. each side.

You will need scissors, glue and sticky tape, a ruler and protractor, cardboard (for your small diamond template and your 8 large 25-diamond guides), colored paper and heavy paper.

1. To make the small diamond template, trace our template (a) onto stiff card – it must be very accurate, as you will use it to make 200 diamonds!

2. To make the small paper diamonds, place your card template onto the colored paper and draw around it.
For the simple star pattern (c), you will need 40 yellow diamonds, 32 red diamonds, 32 orange diamonds and 96 blue diamonds.

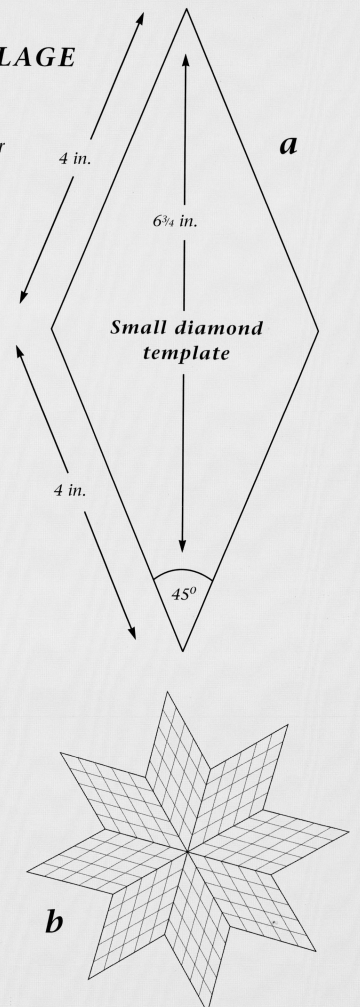

a

4 in.

6¾ in.

Small diamond template

4 in.

45⁰

b

3. Lay 25 small diamonds into a neat diamond shape on a large piece of card. Each side should have 5 small diamonds and will be 20 in. long. This large diamond should have a 45° angle, like template (a). Don't worry about colors, just trace around the shape and then cut it out.

4. Make 8 large diamonds out of strong card, using this big diamond as a guide.

5. Now you can lay out each set of 25 small diamonds onto one of the large diamonds, following the simple star pattern (c). When you have the pattern right, glue the diamonds down. Repeat this for the other 7 diamonds. Each large diamond must be exactly the same – so make sure your first one is correct!

6. To make up the star, you must piece together your 8 large diamonds – follow picture (c). Make sure you have the right points in the middle to make the central star. When you have the pattern right, stick the 8 diamonds together with tape.

7. Paste your star onto a background piece of colored paper, so it looks just like a quilt! Your star collage is ready!

Eagle star quilt

When you have made this star pattern, you might want to try something more adventurous. Try the one above with two eagles in the middle, or design your own!
If you photocopy and enlarge the blank lone star template (b) you can try out different colors and patterns. Once you've made a lone star collage, you may want to try a real quilt. There are many books to show you how and you can use these patterns.

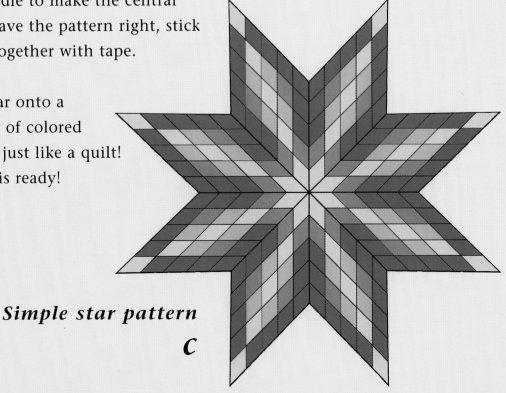

Simple star pattern
c

Shota and her family are Oglala Lakota, members of the Great Sioux Nation. The Sioux are made up of seven "bands" called the "Oceti Sakowin" and speak three dialects: Nakota, Dakota and Lakota. People from the Sioux Nation usually prefer to be called Nakota, Dakota or Lakota, depending on which one they speak. Lakota is still spoken on Pine Ridge Reservation and is taught in schools there. The language in this book is Lakota.

Even those who don't speak the language fluently use lots of Lakota words and sometimes have Lakota names. (Shota's name means "smoke" in Lakota, "Unci" means grandmother and "Takoja" means granddaughter. All names have meanings: Esther means "star" in Hebrew – do you know what your name means?)

In 1800, the Great Sioux Nation dominated the northern plains of America, an area including most of what is now the Dakotas, northern Nebraska, eastern Wyoming and south-eastern Montana. They lived by hunting and buffalo were central to the people's lives. The meat provided food but, once it was killed, no part of the buffalo was wasted: hides were made into everything from moccasin soles to tepee covers, blankets and the very important robes; bones were made into glue; tendons were used for sewing; horns were made into spoons and the head hair was used to stuff pillows.

However, over the next 100 years, settlers gradually moved into the area and in 1868, using the Fort Laramie Treaty, the US Government set up the Great Sioux Reservation and ordered the Sioux people to move there, leaving their homeland to the settlers. The Sioux defeated the U.S. Army several times, but eventually, when the settlers had almost wiped out the buffalo they lived on, the Sioux were forced to give in.

In 1889 the government split the Great Sioux Reservation into six smaller reservations, which were gradually reduced to a tiny fraction of the area where the Sioux once lived free.

Today, about 20,000 Oglala Lakota live on Pine Ridge Reservation and, though many people move to the cities to find work, the Reservation is always "home" and most return regularly to keep up strong family and community ties.

Holidays, and especially pow-wows (wacipi – festivals of singing and dancing) are a popular time for getting together. The annual Pine Ridge pow-wow is held during August, a time of many shooting stars...

As the buffalo numbers were depleted, the Lakota had to find other materials for making bedcovers, clothes and so on. Already skilled at sewing, they adapted the art of quilt making from one of the groups of settlers. Just as the settlers quilted to make use of every piece of old or scrap material, so the Lakota valued it as a way of reusing precious resources – just as they had done in the past with the buffalo.

Unlike European quilters, however, Lakota quilters work alone rather than in groups. They do work together in times of crisis, when quilts have to be produced in a hurry (just like in the story).

The Lakota incorporated many of their traditional symbols into the quilts. Stars, known as the Great Spirit's breath, were often painted on buffalo-hide robes and now the Lakota quilters began to place them at the center of their quilts.

Traditionally in Native American communities, people were not judged by what they owned, but by how much they gave away during their lives. "Give-aways" were used especially to commemorate the dead and buffalo robes played an important part in the ceremony. Gradually, star quilts became central to these memorials, continuing the buffalo-robe tradition.

Over time, star quilts came to be used in all sorts of celebrations, especially the birth of a new baby. They have become an important way of honoring basketball players on reservation high-school teams. During graduation at Red Cloud Indian School on Pine Ridge Reservation, South Dakota, star quilts cover the graduates' chairs and the gymnasium is transformed by the quilts hanging on the walls.

Today stars and star quilts are particularly associated with the Lakota. They have become central to many celebrations and are both a reminder of the past and a means of carrying Lakota traditions into the future.

The star quilt is a powerful symbol, binding the community together and strengthening ties between generations, just like it does in Shota's story...

Folktale Series

Drawing on traditional themes,
Margaret Bateson Hill has written four
beautiful new stories.
In each story, the heroine
uses a local craft to solve her problems
and instructions are included at the back
so children can try it out themselves.

•

Lao Lao of Dragon Mountain
illustrated by Francesca Pelizzoli
with Manyee Wan and Sha Liu Qu

Delicate artwork provides a perfect context
for this beautiful story set in China.
Featuring the full story text in Chinese
and paper-cutting instructions.

•

Shota and the Star Quilt
illustrated by Christine Fowler
with Gloria Runs Close to Lodge

Stunning, naïve artwork beautifully
complements this moving story of
a modern Native American girl.
Featuring the full story in Lakota
and a fantastic collage project.

•

Masha and the Firebird
illustrated by Anne Wilson
with Michael Sarni

Magical artwork enhances a poetic story
of a Russian peasant girl.
Featuring poetry in Russian
and an inspiring egg-painting project.

•

Chanda and the Mirror of Moonlight
illustrated by Karin Littlewood
with Asha Kathoria

Exquisite watercolours capture
the atmosphere of Rajasthan in India.
Featuring the full story in Hindi,
and an engaging mirror-decorating project.

Margaret Bateson Hill was born
and grew up in Lancashire, England.
At University she studied
Drama and English.
Now Margaret spends her days
sharing stories with children and adults
in schools, museums and libraries.

Margaret enjoys meeting people
from different cultures – this, she says,
makes Brixton in South East London
the ideal place to live as it is definitely
one of the cross-roads of our world.

Christine Fowler was born
in Lancashire, England and studied
illustration at Manchester University,
graduating in 1994.
Shota and the Star Quilt was Christine's
first children's picture book.

Gloria Runs Close to Lodge
is a member of the Oglala Lakota tribe
from Pine Ridge, South Dakota and
she currently resides on Wind River
Reservation, Wyoming.

She has worked in all areas of education
for 25 years and currently teaches at
Wyoming Indian High School,
Ethete, Wyoming. Gloria is
a Cultural Facilitator and strongly
believes in bilingual education.

Philomine Lakota Tunweya
Waste Win (Good Scout Woman) is from
the Oceti Sakowin, Seven Campfires.
She comes from the Oglala, Hohwoju,
Itazipaco and Hunkpapa Bands of the
Titatonwan or Teton Band of the Lakota.
Philomine is presently an Instructor
for the Lakota Studies Department of the
Oglala Lakota College on the
Pidge Reservation of South Dakota.

ZERO TO TEN books are available from all good bookstores.

If you have any problems obtaining any title, please contact our distributers:
IPG, 814 North Franklin Street, Chicago, Illinois 60610. Tel: 312 337 0747 Fax: 312 337 5985